Jed's Really Useful Poem

Ragnhild Scamell
Jane Gray

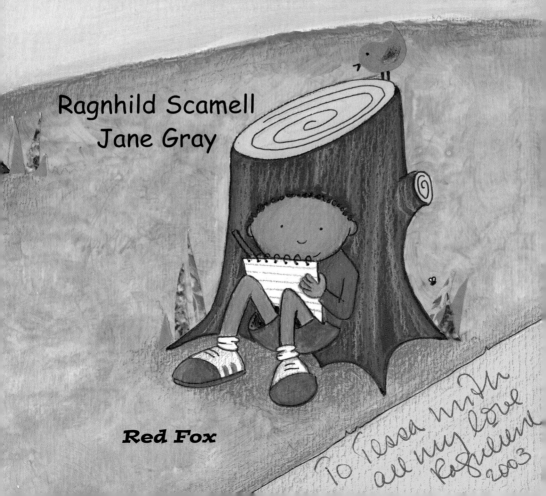

Red Fox

To Tessa with all my love
Ragnhild 2003

The old tree in the park had died. Jed watched the lorry carting it off. All that was left was its large, gnarled stump.

The local paper ran a competition.

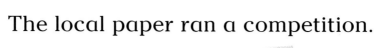

Calling all children.
Would you like to:
Plant a sapling in the park?
Have lunch with the mayor?
Get your name and
photograph in the paper?
Yes?
Then write a poem about trees
and send it to us before next
Saturday.

Yes! thought Jed. I'd like to plant a sapling and have my name and photograph in the paper. But I don't know about having lunch with the mayor. I bet he eats snails and caviar and things like that.

So Jed wrote a poem:

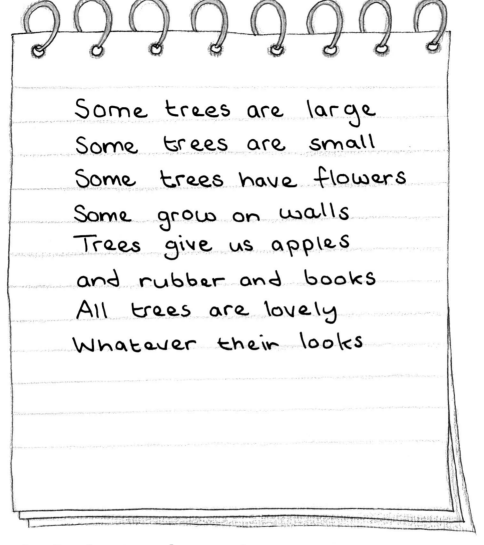

Some trees are large
Some trees are small
Some trees have flowers
Some grow on walls
Trees give us apples
and rubber and books
All trees are lovely
Whatever their looks

At the bottom he wrote:

"P.S. – If my poem wins, please could I have a large burger with extra fries, instead of lunch with the mayor? Love from Jed."

A week later, his mum's mobile rang.
It was the editor of the local paper.
"May I speak with Jed?" she said.

On Wednesday morning, the mayor's gleaming car stood waiting outside Jed's house. Jed bounced out in his brand new trainers and knocked on the window.

The mayor got out of his car and handed
Jed the sapling.

At the park, someone had already dug the hole for the sapling. All Jed had to do was put it in and shovel some soil over its roots.

Snap! went the
photographer.

Now it was time for lunch, and soon Jed, the editor and the mayor were tucking into large burgers with extra fries.

The mayor kicked off his black lace-ups,
and wiggled his toes under the table.

Jed

A week later, Jed's
photograph and poem
were in the paper.

Mum was really, really pleased.
She cut them out and put them
on the fridge door with her best
magnet. She used the rest of
the paper to line the bin.

Grandma, who lived down the road, was all in a flutter when Jed called.

She grabbed the paper, without looking at it. Then she used it to line Betty's basket.

Betty's having her puppies!

Soon a tiny puppy was crawling all over Jed's poem.

"That boy looks a bit like you," said Grandma when she'd found her glasses.

"It *is* me, Grandma," said Jed.

"Clever boy!" said Grandma. "You're almost as clever as Betty."

At school, Jed's teacher had pinned his
poem and photograph up on the wall.

Now she was busy decorating the window with a chain of paper people she'd made out of the rest of the paper.

Soon there seemed to be pictures of Jed everywhere. At the recycling centre . . .

24

On the pond . . .

In the park . . .

Even in Jed's bedroom, where his gerbil made a cosy nest with the newspaper.

BARBECUE

ALL WELCOME!

Every morning, Jed went to water his little sapling. He wanted it to look good for Saturday, because the mayor had invited everyone to a barbecue in the park. Behind Jed, two men were unpacking their tools.

30

The two men began to hammer
and saw the tree stump.

Early on Saturday morning, a van arrived in the park. Two strong men lifted off a new bench and put it by the sapling.

It was very, very heavy.

At two o'clock, the park was full of people, all waiting for the mayor's car. But the mayor had decided not to waste any more petrol and had bought himself a lovely pair of trainers. He arrived, huffing and puffing, but his feet felt good.

What's this?

The mayor picked up his loud-hailer.
"This beautiful bench was Jed's idea. It was
made of wood from the old tree."

Welcome!

Jed looked shy as everyone clapped.
"Now it's time for the surprise," said
the mayor. "You can pull off
the cloth, Lucy!"

"Aaahhh!" said everyone. The old tree stump had become a beautiful birdbath.

SATURDAY 2PM GRAND CELEBRATION BARBECUE

37

Everyone loved the barbecued sausages, and the birds loved the crumbs.
It was a perfect day.

Most people put their rubbish in the bin. But some just chucked theirs. Jed helped the mayor to stuff it all into sacks.

Now it was time to go home. But there was still a newspaper flying around.

Jake caught it and was just about to put it in the bin, when he spotted something.

Another competition:

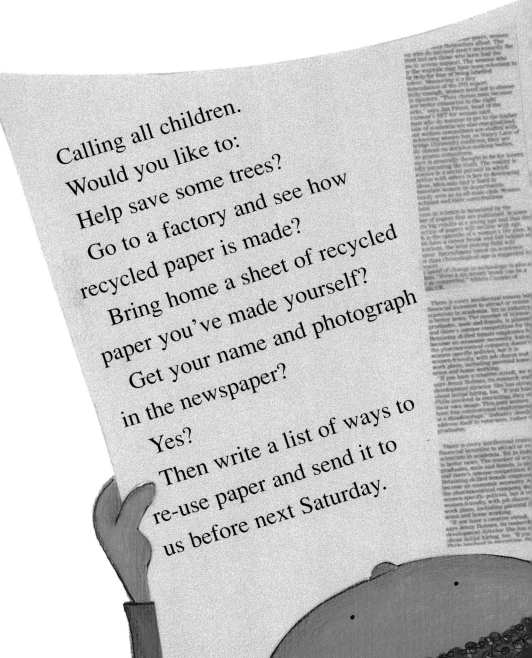

Calling all children.
Would you like to:
Help save some trees?
Go to a factory and see how
recycled paper is made?
Bring home a sheet of recycled
paper you've made yourself?
Get your name and photograph
in the newspaper?
Yes?
Then write a list of ways to
re-use paper and send it to
us before next Saturday.

Jed ran all the way home.

He already had loads of ideas.

Back home, he found an old envelope on his mum's desk.

Then he started to write:

1. Use the back of old envelopes to write on.
2. Line the bin.
3. Line dog's bed.
4. Make paper chains.
5. Wrap parcels.
6. Recycle - bin.
7. Make boats and hats.
8. Put it over your head when the sun shines.
9. Tear it up for your gerbil.
10. . . . .

Jed yawned. He couldn't think of any
more tonight. Tomorrow he'd ask all his
friends.

Recycle paper to make a papier-mâché head that looks like Jed or the mayor.

YOU WILL NEED:

a balloon, 2 cups of water, 1 cup of flour, a bowl, poster paints, newspaper torn into strips, a few strips of cardboard

Day 1:

1. Cover a table with newspaper *(look for any competitions first!)*.

2. Blow up the balloon and tie the end.

3. Mix the flour and water in the bowl to make glue.

4. Dip strips of newspaper in the mixture and stick them on the balloon. *Make sure they're not too wet!* Cover the balloon with about three layers.

5. For the hair, scrunch up bits of newspaper dipped in glue and stick them on top of the balloon.

6. Leave to dry overnight.

Day 2:

1. When the papier-mâché is dry, you can burst the balloon.

2. Paint Jed's face (or the mayor's).

3. Paint Jed's hair (the mayor doesn't have much hair!) and let it dry.

4. Take a few strips of cardboard and stick them together in a circle to make a stand.

Save trees. Use paper wisely.

In fifteen years' time, Jed's sapling will be 2.50 metres tall. If you cut it down, it might be turned into paper. But much of it will be used only once. What a waste! Recycle your old cereal, toy or trainer boxes. Then they can be turned into new paper!

As an old man, Jed might sit under his tree in the park. It would have 250,000 leaves or more. There would be birds singing and squirrels climbing. Jed would be glad it wasn't turned into paper.

Ragnhild Scamell

How did you get the idea for this story? I saw a huge tree lying across the road after a great storm.

Why did you write a story about a tree? I wanted to tell children how important trees are.

Do you have a special tree? Yes, the one that fell over in the storm was special. It had a forked trunk and looked like an elephant.

Do you recycle at your house? Of course! I want to help save the Earth.

Have you ever had lunch with a famous person like the mayor? I once had tea with the Queen. There were lots of other people there, because it was a garden party. I wore a red hat and ate cake and sandwiches. My husband ate ten, because he hadn't had any lunch. I hope the Queen didn't notice.

Have you ever had a poem published in the newspaper? Yes. And, next to it, there was a cartoon of a man with a speech-bubble that said: *Mrs Scamell, you're a winner!*